THE ROARING LION
And Other Stories

Aaron Kalokola

TANZANIA EDUCATIONAL PUBLISHERS LTD

Tanzania Educational Publishers Ltd,
TEPU House,
Uganda Road,
Plot No. 45, Block MDA,
Phone: +255 685 997 583/ +255 758 147 871
Email: tepultd@yahoo.com
Website: www.tepu.co.tz
P.O. Box 1222,
Bukoba, Tanzania.

First Edition, 2003
Second Edition, 2019

Illustrator: Sudi Salum

ISBN 978 9987 671 21 2

TABLE OF CONTENTS

Introduction

For many generations, stories have been told by all tribes on earth. Some are funny, while others are frightening or disturbing. Each story told has a lesson to man or woman so that he or she may develop a moral character.

Stories fall into different categories: there are those about man or woman which basically speak on marriage and traditional rulers: their achievements, failures, cruelty, hunting powers and his ways of life and behaviour. There are those telling about animals. Our forefather's first encountered animals during hunting expeditions. As they observed various animals escaping enemies or stealing crops in the fields, people were able to distinguish clever and foolish animals. In this way they developed stories.

Animals do not speak human language, though tamed ones are able to understand the orders from their masters. For example, a cow going astray is ordered to change course and immediately takes the wanted course. A dog knows its name. When called by its name, it leaves its friends and runs to its master. The only animals that spoke are in scriptures: the Serpent in the Garden of Eden and Baalem's ass. A story can't be interesting unless its characters speak and act. That's why we find animals speaking in our stories.

In Bukoba, Tanzania, stories were told by parents and grandparents to keep children and grandchildren awake for supper, which usually was taken between 8 and 10 p.m. The stories amused children and taught them good behaviour. When village children met, they recited these stories and the latter continued from generation to generation.

Unfortunately, these stories are dying out quickly. A few are in books, which, however, are not read by many children. The latter attend schools and when they come home they have no time to listen to stories because of domestic chores. The students in boarding schools never listen to stories at all, except those in story books written by foreigners. So, young mothers and fathers do not know traditional stories. Radio and televisions have also contributed a great deal to the death of traditional stories. On the other hand, good storytellers have passed away due to old age.

It has taken me time to collect these seven stories. I ask anybody who has a story, whether short or long, to narrate it or write it and pass it to his children. It will be very useful to them and to the coming generations.

Aaron Kalokola

The Roaring Lion

It's common for chiefs, traditional rulers and some political rulers to celebrate their birthdays. Citizens and invited guests gather and show their respects to the chief or the rurer. Food and drinks are served to the guests to celebrate the occassion.

Chief Barige was somehow different from other chiefs. He liked parades to open his birthday feasts.

One day he made a feast for all animals. The latter gathered at the chiefs' parade ground. They all stood at ease, scattered singly and in small groups according to their types. In those days, all animals spoke one language but ate different kinds of food.

Then the chief arrived. He stood on the platform ready to inspect the guard of honour.

"Who is the commander?" The chief asked. The elephant, who is the biggest animal can only whistle. The tallest animal, the giraffe, makes no sound that can be heard.

The Hyena thinks only of chewing bones of left over's when the lion has killed its prey. The Antelope always looks amazed, ready to sprint away when danger smells. Mr. Hippopotamus has no friendship with land walking animals.

The Roaring Lion

The Lion showed up and stood apart. He gathered all the animals in a straight line. "Stand at ease!" Attention. He repeated the same several times and the whole ground was silent. Then, he marched forward to invite the chief to inspect the parade and he did so.

After the inspection, chief Barige, very much impressed, promoted the Lion to the rank of Roaring Lion. He gave him the deepest and most terrifying voice. He made him commander of all animals because he commanded well the Parade of the Chief.

Why Cats live with Men and Monkeys Live in Forests

Once upon a time, a monkey and a cat were great friends. Their friendship was bound up by one common skill, for each of them was able to climb up a tree or a high object fast. A monkey was better than his friend in that he could jump from one tree to the next while the cat to get from one tree to the next nearby, he had first to climb down and start from the bottom.

The two friends lived together in a forest. The cat ate small animals, especially, mice and lizards, while the monkey feed on the fruits that grew high in branches of trees. When looking for food, neither left his friend at a distance. They slept on one tree in well sheltered branches. Seeing the two animals together, one could judge that they lived happily.

Where there is friendship, enemity always seeks interference. The buffalo was their enemy. He hated them so much, that, he always thought of ways to destroy them completely. He could spend a whole day under the tree in which they were resting, hoping they might feel hungry and climb down to get food but such a chance never happened.

One day, as usual, the buffalo was under the tree waiting to fulfill his aching aim. Suddenly, a figure walking on two legs appeared. The two friends wondered much what it was. "Is it an animal?" asked the monkey.

"How can he walk erect?" Replied the cat. "It is your habit, you monkeys, to stand erect as he is doing now, but you can't walk."

At that moment they heard a loud crack! They were so terrified that they almost dropped down. Only their skills held them in the branches. After regaining their senses, they saw the figure pulling away the buffalo. It was dead. They both came down and started jumping with joy for their enemy was no more.

"Now I remember." The monkey told his friend. "This man walks on two legs. He is a hunter. The weapon he uses to kill animals is called a gun. It spits fire and death, that's why the buffalo died.

The Cat nodded in agreement and told his friend, "Man must be good. Let's follow him and see where he lives. Perhaps we may be happy there."

Let's follow the Man

They followed the traces of blood, which ended up in a house. The Cat told his friend, "Let us enter the house."

The Monkey refused and argued, "That man can kill us. We're animals, remember! I'm staying outside here."

The Cat entered the house miaowing, *"Peace! Peace! Peace!"* The woman liked the sound and the man didn't care. She gave it a piece of meat. The meat of the buffalo! After swallowing a part of its enemy, the Cat sat on the lap of the woman miaowing, *"Peace-m-m-m! Peace-m-m-m-! Peace-m-m-m!"*

The Monkey waited for the Cat to come out of the house, but it was in vain. After losing his friend, the Monkey cried, *"Kafe! Kafe!* which means, Die! Die!"* The Monkey wished death on both the Cat and the man.

Since that time, monkeys have lived in the forest, and when they see man, the cry, *"Kafe! Kafe!"* In revenge, Monkeys steal man's crops, while Cats live with man in peace, helping him to kill mice which destroy his crops and other belongings.

Chapter 3

The Leopard and the Luck Monkey

Friendship is an association of two persons. It is love among people of the same or different sex. This may come automatically when people meet or cooperate in business, herding, hunting, fishing or organizing ceremonies. However, others practice friendship in evil ways like theft and the like.

In the past, places like Bukoba, friendship was comented by involving their blood. Two people make small cuts on each partner's umbilicus. Then, cooked robust coffee cherries were rubbed on the blood from the cuts. Each ate his fellow's blood on those cherries. After this act, these two persons, wewe, without question, true brothers by blood.   No member of these two families could take a wife or husband from the other side. Such friendship was called *Omukago*, to mean friendship cemented by blood. If a grandchild would do so, then he was required to pay to the elders a he-goat as a token of burying the friendship made by those ancestors.

On the other hand, long ago, it was believed that a Monkey and a Leopard were friends. They worked together. The monkey would show his friend where animals for food were hiding and the Leopard would show the monkey where fruits were available. They shared each other's problems.

It happended that in one year, in the past, a great drought struck the area where the Monkey and the Leopard lived. There was a big scarcity of food. The Leopard failed to kill animals, for they had ran away to distant places where better conditions provided them enough food. The Monkey jumped from tree to tree to get at least dry fruits.

After missing food for a long time, the Leopard said to himself, "I must go to the Monkey and ask him to eat him up. In this way I can live longer."

So, the Leopard went to his intimate friend, the Monkey. On seeing the Leopard, the Monkey knew at once that his friend was dying of hunger, for his eyebrows had swollen. A hungry one is known by swollen eyebrows.

The Leopard told his friend, the Monkey, "I have gone everywhere to get an animal to eat; but I have failed. It is now many days since I had food. Please, my friend, help me. Let me eat you up so that I may live longer."

The Monkey was surprised by his friend's request. He told him in reply, "My friend, you see I am only bones. I have missed food for a very long time, too. Let's go to a tall tree and I will show you how to solve your problem."

The Monkey settled on the highest branch

The Leopard was very much pleased, hoping to get food soon. They both went towards a tall tree. There, the Monkey told the Leopard, "Please throw me up three times. When I fall down the third time, I'll be fat enough to be eaten."

The Leopard was very happy. He threw the Monkey up with all his might. Golden chance comes but once! On being thrown up, the Monkey caught a branch of the tall tree. It then started climbing high on the tree and settled on the highest branch. He then barked strongly at the Leopard, "Friendship! Friendship! Is this what it means? Miserable!"

The Elephant and the Tricky Hare

One day a Lion, the King, made a party to celebrate his birthday. Invitations were sent to all animals so that they could attend the occasion.

On that day, all animals went to the Lion to share the happiness with their King. They ate and drank as much as their stomachs could hold. After that, the King announced a prize to be given to the one who could dance best.

One of the King's sons started the dance. He blew a whistle and all the animals began dancing. The baboon was drumming, for he was good at it. For each dance, he used a different style. From the beginning to the end the King and his quests were quite amused.

At the end, the Hare was announced the winner, for he danced finely throughout. The King gave him a beautiful reward.

On the way home the Elephant asked the Hare, "How were you able to dance so nicely without feeling tired? What can I do to dance as nicely as you?"

The Hare answered, "You are very fat. Every part of your body is very fatty. You can't jump. You can't twist. You can't bend. In order to help you, let me cut off part of your thighs. I'll send you medicine to heal the wound quickly."

The Elephant agreed. The Hare cut off meat from the Elephant's thighs. He took the meat home, roasted it, and ate it. He then went out into the grassland and found a tall tree. In the branches he hid a heavy rock. After doing this, the Hare returned to his home.

The Hare didn't send any medicine and the Elephant's body began to decay.

The Elephant sent Antelope to the Hare to ask for the medicine. The Hare was very pleased. He told the Antelope to follow him to a certain tree and said, "The medicine is high up in this tree. In order to take it, lie under the tree on your back, close your eyes, open your mouth, I will drop medicine into it and then run away quickly with it.

The Antelope agreed and followed the instructions. The Hare climbed up and dropped the rock on the Antelope's head. He died. The Hare laughed happily and took the carcass home to eat its meat.

The Elephant's condition was getting worse. He sent Hyena, Monkey, and Gazelle, one at a time, to the Hare who repeated the same messae cto each of them and all died and were eaten up by the Hare. In the end, Leopard volunteered to go and see what was wrong with the Hare.

On arrival, the Hare gave him the same instructions, but when the Leopard lay under the tree, he only opened his mouth. He didn't completely close his eyes. When the rock dropped, he moved away his head, and pretended he was dead. The Hare tied the Leopard as usual and carried him away on his head. On the way, the Leopard pinched the Hare. The Hare dropped the Leopard with a loud bang and ran away.

On the way, the Hare thought how he would enter his house. "May be the Leopard took a short cut and hid in my house." He thought. He got an idea and went on.

When he reached his house, he stood outside and called, "My house! My house!" There was silence. He called again, "My house! My house!" Again, it was silence.

He shouted, "Now I know. There is somebody in my house, for whenever I come back and call out, my house responds."

My House! My House!

The Hare called again, "My house! My house!"
"Here I am," a voice called from the house. It was the
Leopard. The Hare ran away laughing.

Chapter 5

All Swallowing Animals Must Stop Swallowing

Snakes have no teeth, so they don't chew food. How then do they eat? They use their mouths to catch insects, mice, lizard, or small fish and swallow them whole.

Pythons are long, larger snakes. They use their strong tails to knock down animals, sometimes even people. They wrap coils of their bodies around what they have caught and squeeze the coils, breaking the bones of the prey. They then swallow the latter.

One day a Toad was hopping slowly, coming from a meeting. On the way home he met a snake. The snake pretended to be friendly to the Toad.

"Where are you coming from, Mr. Toad?" the snake asked.

The Toad answered, "King Lion called a meeting of all animals and I'm sorry you didn't attend."

"Yes, I didn't," Replied the snake and added, "My wife has given birth and I have been nursing her. What was the meeting about? Please stay and tell me."

The Toad hopped away

Instead, the Toad hopped away as fast he could go. After covering a long distance, he stopped and said to the snake, "All swallowing animals must stop that habit right now. That's has been decided at the meeting."

Then he hopped away and disappeared among the stones.

Chapter **6**

Why Leopards Eat Dogs

In those days, a Leopard and a Dog were great friends. As both were fresh eaters, they hunted animals together for food. The Leopard was stronger and more intelligent than his friend. On the other hand, the Dog knew the trails of the animals and barked on seeing one. They continued living together like this for a long time.

One day, the Leopard got a fiancee. Her parents needed dowry. He was asked to collect a bucketful of winged termites. The latter fly from their anthills in February and early in March. In April and May, they fly from holes in the ground. In both seasons it is their time for making nests and producing more termites. In Bukoba, winged termites are food for people. Plenty of them are collected in February. A pithole is dug at the foot of the anthill, then a shade is placed to cover the anthill in total darkness. At the time of flight, the termites find no way out and gather in the pithole. When the flight is over, they are collected and placed in a container.

The Leopard collected the termites in mid February. He was helped by his friend, the Dog.

They had a good collection. They cooked the

insects and dried them over a fire to give them a fine taste. They made a banana fiber container called *Omushenga,* filled it with a bucketful of termites, and they went to pay dowry.

The Dog opened the "Omushenga"

All the time after cooking and drying the termites, the dog was troubled at heart. "Why has my friend failed to give me even a sourceful to eat? Imagine all this work, I'll teach him a lesson."

The Dog was carrying the *Omushenga.* After covering a distance, the Dog told his friend that he was going for a long call in the nearly bush with the

Omushenga and he would take care of the same there. While in the bush, the Dog opened the *Omushenga* and ate a quarter of the termites. Then he filled the empty space with his stool. When the Leopard saw that his friend was delaying in returning, he sang through his nose:

> *Shit! Shit! Shit!*
> *Shitting the habit*
> *of dogs worldwide.*
> *You shit and eat*
> *Human shit wherever it is.*

The Dog heard the song and answered back through his nose:

> *Pay stool! Pay stool!*
> *Shame and shame.*
> *The girl off. The girl off.*
> *Laugh and cry await ahead.*

The Dog returned, joined his friend and continued carrying the container, which was now partly filled with termites and partly filled with his stool.

On arriving at the residence of the Leopard's in laws-to-be, they were warmly welcomed. The container was received with both hands and put at a well-prepared place. After greetings, the Dog told his friend silently that he was going for a long call. He went out and didn't come back.

Meanwhile, some neighbours and relatives who were invited for the occasion came singing happily to see the son-in-law-to-be and to cheer the dowry.

On opening the *Omushenga*, they couldn't believe their eyes. Stool poured out first. All who were there held sticks. They beat the Leopard severely and the Leopard returned home weeping bitterly. On the way he didn't see the Dog, but promised to eat him wherever he sees him.

To this day, Leopards eat Dogs, remembering the shame done to their forefather.

The Partridge and the Ungrateful Snake

A Partridge lives alone in the grasslands. Animals and birds do not grow crops for their food. They just go about in search of food and shelter.

One day, the Partridge was eating flying termites at the anthill. A Snake was also eating the same. The Snake liked the beauty of the bird and moved near. They continued eating the insects together. The Partridge was about to leave when the Snake asked him to stay and make friendship.

From that time the Partridge had a friend, the Snake. They stayed together, they talked and walked everywhere in the grassland. Sometimes they came near people's houses, but they ran away on seeing a person. They ate insects and when they could not get enough, they shared what was caught. But the Partridge ate seeds also, so he grew more beautiful and fatter than his friend.

One early evening, they were resting on a flat stone waiting for the night. The Snake said to his friend, "Let's study each other's inside of our mouthparts." The bird agreed, and opened its mouth while the Snake looked inside.

"Did you see anything?" asked the Partridge. "No, I didn't. You're really beautiful, my friend," answered the Snake.

The Snake wrapped itself around the Partridge's neck

Then, the Snake opened its mouth and the Partridge looked inside it. "What did you see?" asked the Snake.

"I saw a black spot in the throat," answered the Partridge.

The Snake didn't say anything. They went to rest for the night. They continued as friends for a long time.

One dry season, they were in the middle of tall grass. Fire blown by strong winds moved toward them. The Snake was afraid and told his friend, "Please let me coil on your neck and then you fly away with me to the hills, or else the fire will kill us."

"The Partridge agreed. The Snake wrapped himself around the bird's neck and they flew at high speed to a hill. They landed safely on a big rock, but the Snake refused to get off the neck of his friend. The Snake asked the latter, "Do you remember one evening when we looked at each other's inside of our mouthparts?"

"Yes, I remember," replied the bird.

"What did you see?" asked the Snake.

"I saw a black spot," the Partridge answered.

"Yes." Said the Snake. That spot is called *Akabajoka,* which means 'bad attitude.' In our family, we hold tightly to what we chance to find. So, today I'm eating you and did that.